Once Upon a Time

A Collection of Classic Fairytales for Kids 4-10

INTRODUCTION

Once upon a time, children around the world were captivated by classic fairytales, transported to enchanted kingdoms and heroic quests by timeless tales of courage, love, and adventure.

Now, with "Once Upon a Time: A Collection of Classic Fairytales for Kids," a new generation can discover these beloved stories for themselves, bringing to life the magical worlds of Cinderella, The Ugly Duckling, Sleeping Beauty, The Frog Prince, and The Three Little Pigs.

With amazing illustrations and engaging storytelling, this collection offers a glimpse into the rich tradition of children's literature, offering a world of imagination and wonder that will captivate young readers and ignite their love of storytelling for years to come.

So gather around and join us on a journey through time and space, where anything is possible and anything can happen - all you need is a little bit of imagination and a love of classic fairytales!

CONTENTS PAGE

Chapter 1: The Ugly Duckling

Chapter 2: The Frog Prince

Chapter 3: The Three Little Pigs

Chapter 4: Sleeping Beauty

Chapter 5: Cinderella

Chapter 1: The Ugly Duckling

Once upon a time, in a quiet little pond,

A mother duck sat, waiting for her offspring to respond.

One by one, the eggs hatched, and out came some cute little ducklings,

But one was different, with feathers brown and ugly, unlike its siblings.

The mother duck loved them all, but the other ducks teased,

And bullied the little brown one.

Feeling sad and blue, it wandered alone.

Wondering why it was different, and what it could do.

The little duckling grew up, still feeling out of place,

Hoping one day, it would find its own space.

It wandered far and wide, through fields and farms,

Until it came across a group of swans, with grace and charm.

The swans welcomed the duckling with open wings,

And to everyone's surprise, the little brown duckling transformed.

Its ugly brown feathers, now pure and white,

And the other ducks were now envious of its sight.

The little brown duckling looked at its reflection,

And saw a beautiful swan, with no objection.

Finally, it found a place where it belonged,

And its heart was filled with happiness and song.

So, my friend, don't judge a book by its cover,

Beauty lies within, and it's important to understand that.

The little ugly duckling found its true worth,

And lived happily ever after, with a new family.

Chapter 2: The Frog Prince

Once upon a time, in a big kingdom so far away,

There lived a stunning princess, who loved to play.

One day while wandering in the woods,

She was stunned as she stumbled upon a frog.

The frog spoke to her and begged her for help.

To turn back to his real self.

He was a prince, cursed by a wicked witch,

And needed the princess's kiss to break the curse.

The princess, being kind-hearted, agreed.

She gave the frog a kiss to fulfill his need.

To her greatest surprise, the frog turned into a very handsome prince,

With a smile so charming, she couldn't imagine.

The prince was grateful and thanked the princess with all his heart.

He asked her to be his bride.

The princess, however, was unsure,

For she had only known him for a little while.

The prince understood and asked for a chance.

To prove his love and make their love magical.

The princess agreed and after some months,

He swept her off her feet with grand gestures and love.

The prince won the princess's heart, with blessings from above.

Together, they ruled the kingdom with love and pride.

They lived happily ever after, with nothing to hide.

So, my friend, true love can break any spell,

And bring happiness and joy, till the very end.

Chapter 3: The Three Little Pigs

A long time ago, in a far, far away land,

Three little pigs set out to make their houses.

They built their houses with different materials in mind,

Straws, sticks, and bricks.

The first little piggy built his small house with straws,

He built it in a hurry with no care.

Unfortunately, one evening, a big bad wolf came around.

He huffed and puffed,

And blew his house down, leaving him sad.

The second little pig built his own house with many sticks,

A little better, he thought, but the wolf came with better tricks.

The big bad wolf huffed and puffed and blew it down,

Leaving the piggy frowning.

The third little pig was wise and clever,

He built his house with bricks that lasted forever.

The wolf came and tried to huff and puff,

But the house stood strong.

The wolf tried to climb down the chimney with a grin.

But the little pig outsmarted him.

The wolf ran away, never to return.

The third little pig jumped into the air filled with joy.

So, my friend, with hard work and determination,

You can overcome any challenge till the very end.

The third little pigs learned it, and so should we.

That's the moral of the story.

Chapter 4: Sleeping Beauty

Once upon a time, in a castle so magnificent,

A baby princess was born with a fate unplanned.

Sadly, a wicked, angry, and mean fairy,

Cursed the princess to hurt her finger on a spinning wheel's spindle.

After which, she will die.

The king and queen were heartbroken and sad.

So, they banned all the spinning wheels to avoid anything bad.

But on her sixteenth birthday, the curious and bold princess,

Found a spinning wheel.

She touched it as if it was gold.

Suddenly, she fell into a deep sleep, so peaceful and sound,

The kingdom slept with her, as the curse bound.

A hundred years passed, with the castle hidden away,

Until a brave prince came around.

He saw the sleeping beauty, so beautiful and fair.

The prince was troubled and knew he had to wake her up.

So, he leaned in and kissed her with a heart so true.

Suddenly, the princess woke up with a lovely smile.

The curse was broken, and the kingdom came to life,

With joy and happiness, ending all strife.

The prince and the beautiful princess fell deeply in love at first sight.

They got married and lived happily ever after, with everything right.

So, my friend, true love kiss,

Can break any curse and make a happy ending.

That's the moral of the story.

Chapter 5: Cinderella

A long time ago, in a faraway land,

There lived a girl with a dream so beautiful.

She wished to go to the ball party and dance with the prince.

But her wicked stepmother gave her no chance.

Cinderella kept working hard every day.

Cleaning and cooking, with no time to play.

Although she never gave up on her dream.

However, in her heart, it was gradually fading away.

But one day, a fairy godmother appeared

With magic and wonders.

She gave Cinderella a beautiful dress

And glass slippers.

The fairy godmother told her to return

Before the clock strikes twelve.

Filled with excitement, Cinderella went to the party.

She danced with the prince with great pleasure.

But when it was almost twelve, she ran home quietly.

Little did she know that she left her beautiful glass slipper behind.

The prince searched the kingdom to find

The girl who left the slipper behind.

Unfortunately, he couldn't find her.

Cinderella's stepmother and stepsisters denied

That she was the one who danced.

But when the slipper fit Cinderella's foot,

The prince knew his search was over.

He took her away to his castle and they lived happily ever after.

QUESTIONS TO ANSWER

1. How did the little brown duckling feel when it was teased and bullied by the other ducks?

2. How does the transformation of the little brown duckling teach readers about the importance of self-acceptance and not judging others based on appearance?

3. How did the princess feel about the frog at first, and what made her decide to give him a kiss to break the curse?

4. What does her decision reveal about her character?

5. What is the importance of building a strong foundation in life, as illustrated by the third little pig's house made of bricks?

6. What does the story teach us about the consequences of making decisions without proper planning and consideration, as seen with the first two little pigs' houses made of straws and sticks?

7. What other lessons can be learned from the story of Sleeping Beauty?

8. How did the curse on Sleeping Beauty come to be?

9. What does Cinderella's story teach us about determination and never giving up on our dreams?

10. What lesson can we learn from the character of the fairy godmother in the story?

www.ingramcontent.com/pod-product-compliance
Ingram Content Group UK Ltd.
Pitfield, Milton Keynes, MK11 3LW, UK
UKHW031318070125
3988UKWH00033B/304